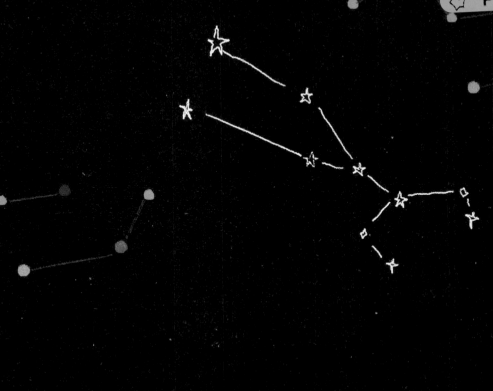

For Aunt Peggy and Aunt Cindy,
who inspire me with their love and their
commitment to children everywhere
—DH

For Sandy,
and for those before us who
paved the way for our freedom to love
—BH

To Mama Paz and Mama Carin,
for teaching me how to love without bounds
—IG

little bee books
an imprint of Bonnier Publishing USA

251 Park Avenue South, New York, NY 10010
Text copyright © 2019 by Daniel Haack and Isabel Galupo
Illustrations copyright © 2019 by Becca Human
All rights reserved, including the right of reproduction in whole or in part in any form.
Little Bee Books is a trademark of Bonnier Publishing USA, and associated colophon
is a trademark of Bonnier Publishing USA.
Manufactured in China HH 1218
First Edition 10 9 8 7 6 5 4 3 2 1
Library of Congress Cataloging-in-Publication Data | Names: Haack, Daniel, author. | Galupo, Isabel,
author. | Human, Becca, illustrator. | Title: Maiden & princess / by Daniel Haack and Isabel Galupo;
illustrated by Becca Human. | Other titles: Maiden and princess | Description: First edition. | New
York, NY: Little Bee Books, [2019] | Summary: When a maiden reluctantly attends a ball for her friend,
the prince, everyone considers her his perfect match until she surprises them — and herself — by
finding true love with someone else. | Identifiers: LCCN 2018026930 | Subjects: | CYAC: Stories in rhyme.
Love — Fiction. | Princesses — Fiction. | Princes — Fiction. | Kings, queens, rulers, etc. — Fiction.
Lesbians — Fiction. | Fairy tales. | BISAC: JUVENILE FICTION / Fairy Tales & Folklore / Adaptations.
JUVENILE FICTION / Stories in Verse. | Classification: LCC PZ8.3.H1125 Mai 2019 | DDC [E] — dc23 | LC
record available at https://lccn.loc.gov/2018026930
ISBN: 978-1-4998-0776-9

littlebeebooks.com
bonnierpublishingusa.com
glaad.org

A PROUD PARTNERSHIP BETWEEN

glaad + Bonnier Publishing USA

A portion of the proceeds from the sale of this
book will be donated to accelerating
LGBTQ acceptance.

Maiden & Princess

WORDS BY Daniel Haack & Isabel Galupo

ART BY Becca Human

little bee books

Once in a faraway kingdom,
a call was made to all.
To find their son a worthy bride,
the king and queen would host a ball.

The ladies in the village
were happy to be invited . . .

except for one young maiden,
who wasn't that excited.

This maiden was quite special,
the bravest in all the land.
She knew the prince from battle,
giving her the upper hand.

"The prince is smart and strong,"
she confided in her mother.
"But if I'm being honest,
I see him as a brother."

Her mother said, "Just go!
And have a bit of fun.
The prince might not be right,
but you could meet the one."

So the maiden put on a gown
and headed to the ball.

She marveled at all the people
who filled the sparkling hall!

The villagers flocked over
to the young maiden's side
and insisted that she
would make the best royal bride.

Even the king and queen
approached her with a smile.

"You must come see our son
and dance with him awhile!"

The maiden was quite flustered,
and so she said, with care,
"Please pardon me, Your Majesties,
but I must get some air."

She fled up to the balcony and looked out at the sky.
A future with the prince made her want to cry.

"I don't mean to bother you," said a voice soft and kind,
"but you seem quite upset. May I ask what's on your mind?"

A beautiful girl emerged
who took the maiden's breath away.
She sat down close to the maiden,
and asked if she could stay.

Soon the maiden had forgotten
about the prince and his throne.
Summoning all her courage,
she took the girl's hands in her own.

Then the doors burst open —
the king and queen walked through.
"There's our precious daughter.
We've looked all over for you!"

The maiden's jaw fell open.
Her head was feeling light.
She had fallen for the *princess*
on this wondrous, starry night.

The royal couple could feel the magic in the air.

The queen said to the king,
"They're the perfect pair!"

The maiden felt quite bashful,
but quickly stole a glance.
She saw the princess smiling
and asked her, "Want to dance?"

They held each other close
as they spun across the floor.
And when they shared a kiss?
Their hearts began to soar.

Soon the maiden and the princess
were seldom seen apart.
They filled their days together
with books, laughter, and art.

They rode horses and sang
and picked wildflowers at dawn.
They practiced their aim
and faced adventure head-on.

When the day finally came
to prove their love was true,
the maiden and the princess
happily said, "I do."